Big-Hearted Charlie Learns How to Make Friends

Book 3

By Krista Keating-Joseph
Illustrated by Phyllis Holmes

ALSO BY KRISTA KEATING-JOSEPH

Big-Hearted Charlie Runs The Mile
Book 1
Royal Palm Literary Award Winner

Big-Hearted Charlie Never Gives Up:
Fun Adventures
Book 2

•••••••••

Big-Hearted Charlie
Learns How to Make Friends
Book 3

ISBN: 978-1-7322135-0-0

Published by
Legacies & Memories
St. Augustine, Florida

(888) 862-2754
www.LegaciesandMemoriesPublishing.com

Contact the Author
Website: www.KristaKeatingJoseph.com
E-mail: kkeatingjoseph@gmail.com

Big-Hearted Charlie Learns How to Make Friends

This is a Story About a Boy
with the Biggest Heart...

Charlie is nervous about starting a new school.
"Charlie, are you ready for your first day?"
his mother asks.
"Mom, what if I can't make any friends?"
"I know you will, you have a big smile and a big heart.
Why wouldn't anyone want to be your friend?"
she says.

As Charlie's mom drops him off at school,
he looks back at her and smiles.
"I do love a challenge and I'm sure it's
not that hard to make a friend," he says.

After school, Mom parks the car and walks to the classroom to meet Charlie. She absolutely loves seeing him exit from his classroom with a HUGE smile and a "I can't wait to tell you expression" on his face.

The door opens and the other kids are streaming out.

Where is Charlie? Usually, Charlie is first and exploding from the room. Mom looks over the other children and sees the top of his head looking down. She is puzzled.

Charlie makes his way to mom
and gives her a big hug.
"Is something wrong? she asks.
How did your first day go?
Do you like your teacher?"
Charlie looks up with his big quiet
blue eyes, "I like Mr. Hanlon,
but I didn't make any friends.
I tried to meet some friends
on the playground, but one of them
said something that hurt my feelings."

"Oh Charlie, I'm so sorry.

I'm sure it was just a tease."

"No, mom, it didn't feel like it.

Does my face look like

it was smashed in an elevator?"

Shocked, his mom first did not know what to say.

Then after a moment she said,

"Charlie, there is NO way you look like that.

That is the strangest thing I have ever heard."

"I was trying to find someone to play

soccer with me and asked a boy

if he wanted to play. He told me my face

looked like it was smashed in an elevator."

"What did you do?"

"I just took my soccer ball and kicked

it around the field by myself."

"Do you want me to let the teacher

know what the boy said to you?"

"No, mom. I can handle it. I'm just not sure how."

Grandma is bringing over some of her
unfinished artwork for her new book.
"Hi Grandma!"
"How was your first day at school?" she asks.
Charlie's mom interrupts. "Grandma, can you
maybe talk to Charlie about friends?
He is having a hard time trying to overcome
something a boy said that was not very nice."

"Sure, Charlie why don't we talk about friends?"
Grandma says, moving to the corner.
She shows him her new pictures laying
on the table where there is also a plate of cookies.

"Look at this picture, Charlie. What if all
the flowers in the world are just roses?"

"The world would miss all these
beautiful smells and color!"

"What if whales were the only living thing swimming in the ocean?"

"Most importantly, Charlie, what if everyone looks
alike and they are all the same?"
"I guess I wouldn't have to worry
about this boy," says Charlie.

"But you wouldn't have all the different types of personalities, traditions, ideas and everything that make this world so special."

"Maybe you should try to find one good
thing in this boy, even if he has not
been very nice to you. He might see
how big-hearted and fun you are."
"Grandma, I love you." Charlie gives her a big
hug as he stuffs a few cookies in his mouth.

The next morning mom catches
Charlie looking in the mirror.
"Is something wrong?"
"I was just seeing if my face
looks squished or something."
"Oh, Charlie, please don't worry.
The one thing I learned
in school is, if you show
that something bothers you,
others will tease you more about it.
Try laughing at yourself. I'll bet they
will have nothing to say after that!"

At school, Charlie ran into the boy.
"Hey, there's the new kid with
the funny face," the boy said, pointing.

Charlie was ready.
"Yea, look at it.... I can do lots of
things with my face. See?"
The boy seems surprised,
but he did not say anything else.

In the afternoon, Charlie goes to exercise class.

The teacher is getting the children

ready for field day.

Charlie is going to run the longest

race of two big laps around the field.

The runners are lined up and ready to go.

At the beginning of the second lap,

Charlie is half-way around

the field and winning by a lot!

As he comes across the finish line,

many children notice him.

"Wow, he's a good runner!"

"Who is that?" "Is he the new boy?"

Charlie smiles and looks back.
First, he sees a group of runners
crossing the finish line. Then he looks
farther... "Wait, who is that?"
There is a boy far behind
and he is last. His head is down
and he looks like he is crying.
This is the boy who
wasn't very nice to Charlie.

Big-Hearted Charlie runs toward the boy.
"Hey do you want me to run in with you?
I don't mind." The boy barely looks up.
"Sure." He is breathing hard, but he
doesn't say anything else.

He and Charlie run the rest of the way in.

They slap hands after crossing the finish line.

"Ur, thanks Charlie," the boy says.

At the end of the day, mom is worried
as she waits by the door of his classroom.

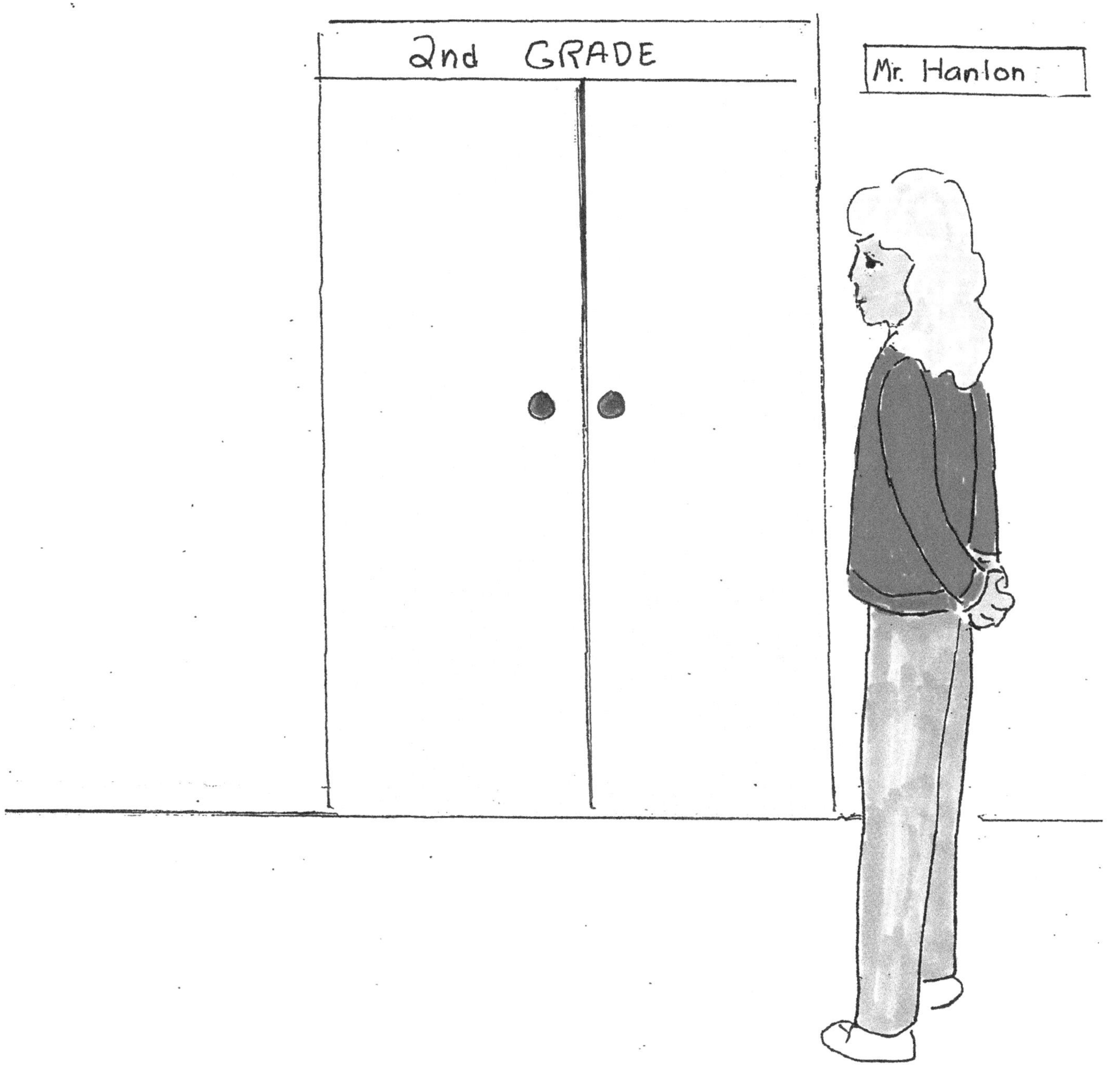
2nd GRADE
Mr. Hanlon

The door flies open
and out bursts Charlie with the biggest smile,
the brightest eyes and the biggest heart...with his
new friend holding Charlie's soccer ball by his side.

Charlie continued to make many
new friends in high school,
in college, and as a U.S. Navy SEAL
traveling all over the world.

Acknowledgments

"Big-Hearted Charlie"

Charlie, with his friend, Jeremy, his stepbrother.

Special thanks to Kelly Valentine Photography; my daughter, Ali; my husband, Ron; and my father, Bill Holmes, for their patience; and to Collin, Nate, Holly, and Jordan for their friendship. Of course, to Charlie, never forgotten.

– *Krista Keating-Joseph*

Contact Krista Keating-Joseph
Website: www.KristaKeatingJoseph.com
E-mail: kkeatingjoseph@gmail.com

CPSIA information can be obtained
at www.ICGtesting.com
Printed in the USA
BVHW02s2153140518
516277BV00018B/181/P